CRITTER
The Class Cat

CRITTER
The Class Cat

Colleen Stanley Bare

G.P. Putnam's Sons • New York

To Pattie Cooper

ACKNOWLEDGMENTS

The author wishes to thank teachers Pattie Cooper, Connie Tate, Carol Parks, and all of the staff at Crowell Elementary School in Turlock, California. Special thanks go to student helpers Sharlet Adamzadeh, Jeff Benton, Carin Cooper, Richard Desper, Jean Hammons, Daniel Hughes, Sarah Manley, Chris Mesa, Angelea Murray, Veronica Romero, and Joyce Williams.

Library of Congress Cataloging-in-Publication Data
Bare, Colleen Stanley.
Critter, the class cat / Colleen Stanley Bare.   p.   cm.
Summary: Relates the adventures of Critter,
the cat who lives in a classroom and belongs
to all the children.
1. Cats—Juvenile fiction.   [1. Cats—Fiction.
2. Schools—Fiction.]   I. Title.
PZ10.3.B243Cr   1989   [E]—dc19
88-6947   CIP   AC
ISBN 0-399-21710-X

Critter is a cat,
but not just
the usual
common,
ordinary,
everybody's
everyday
kind of cat.

Critter is an uncommon, unusual,
extraordinary *class cat.*

Critter belongs to all of the children in a school class.

He lives at the school, so most of what he does, he does at the school.

He lies on the
children's desks
at school.

He eats at school out of his
own dish.

He sits on the teacher's desk,
and sleeps under it.

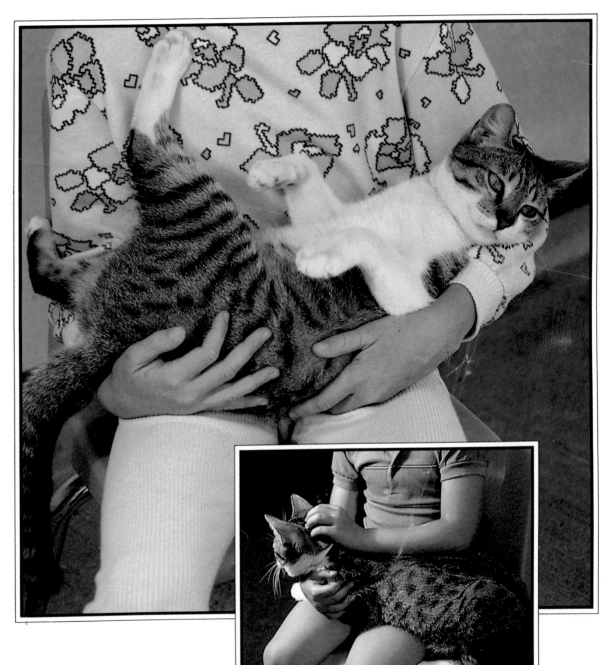

He lies on laps.

Critter plays at school—
with crayons,
pencils, paper,
erasers, string,
balls, backpacks,
and shoes.

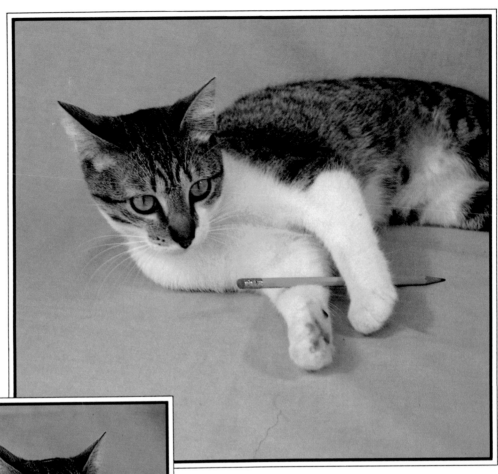

Sometimes he has his teeth brushed
at school, by the teacher.

He rests on the school grass.

He climbs a school tree and
chews on the branches.
But when someone calls
"Here, Critter,"…

he comes
down in
a hurry.

And at night, when the classroom
  is empty, dark, and silent,
Critter curls up in his cozy
  box-bed and sleeps at school.

He only leaves the school on
  weekends and vacations, when
  he goes to the teacher's house.
He rides in her car and wears a
  seat belt.

Critter
is a safe
cat.

The children
cuddle Critter.

The children
pat Critter.

The
children
hug
Critter.

At Christmastime he has his
very own party, with a
plate of goodies and special
Critter Christmas presents.

Critter opens his
Christmas gifts:
cans of tuna,
tasty cat treats,
balls, stuffed toys,
a pillow for his
box-bed.

Sometimes
the
children
dress up
Critter,

in fancy
clothes,
and in
funny
hats.

One day something mysterious happens. A lunch bag is torn open but only one thing is taken: a tuna sandwich.

Who would steal a tuna sandwich from a school lunch?

Who indeed!
Critter loves tuna.

Does Critter learn the class lessons?

Well—

Can Critter count?

The children think he can.

One ball
Two balls
Three balls.

Can Critter read?

Sometimes he seems to try.

Can Critter color?
He appears to
    think about it.

Can Critter compute?

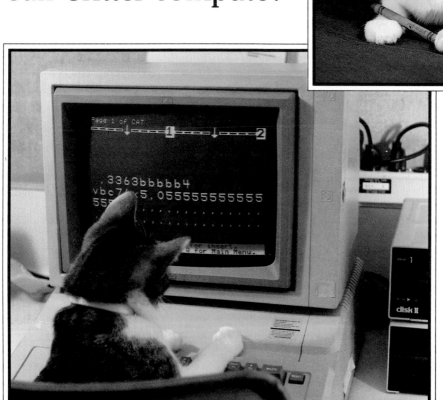

Perhaps he pretends.

But what Critter does best
is to watch and look,
and watch and observe,
and watch and watch and watch.
Every day he watches.

He watches
the children
write.

He watches
the children
read.

He watches the children color.

He watches
the children
compute.

He watches
the children
play on the
playground.

From Critter the children
have learned cat care,
not to hurt or tease,

and to
be gentle,
kind, and
loving.

And from the children Critter has
learned human care, not to
bite or scratch, and to be a calm,
patient, well-behaved, smart
class cat.